FILE COPY

THE WAY HOME

by Judith Benét Richardson · pictures by Salley Mavor

The Bodley Head
London

To Peter and Ian
(and for Molly and Judy-Sue)

Savi went down to the beach with her mother.

They splashed and rolled in the water.
Then Savi played with her boat.

Her mother cooled off in the shade
of a banana tree and ate bananas.
She rolled her big body from side to side
in the sand.

Savi stayed in the water.

The hot sun slid down and made long shadows
stretch out in front of the banana trees.

"Now it's time to go home," rumbled Savi's mother.

Savi sucked in another trunkful of water.

"Time to go home," grumbled her mother, more loudly.

Savi squirted water into her boat to see if it would sink.

"*Time to go home,*" trumpeted her mother.

"No, no, no," squealed Savi, waving her trunk back and forth. "No, no, no."

And she stayed as far out in the water as she could.

Her mother stamped her feet and trumpeted, but Savi did not come.

So the big elephant turned around and walked off
through the long shadows of the banana trees.

The sun went down a little farther.
Savi came out of the water and lay on her towel.
She began to feel cold and hungry.

A star appeared in the sky.
Then Savi saw a pale shape in the grass.
Was it the new moon lying there?
Was it an elephant's toenail?
No, it was a banana.

Savi picked it up. As she did, she saw
another banana just beyond the first banana . . .

and beyond it another, and
beyond that still another.

Savi followed the banana trail,
eating as she went.

When she got to the end of the trail, and all
the bananas were gone, there was her mother!
Savi ran to her.

Savi looked up and saw, high over her mother's head, one last banana.

She stretched and stretched her trunk, but she could not reach it.

"Please pick the last banana for me," she said.

"That banana is the moon," said her mother. "It will help us to see our way home."

Savi curled her trunk around her mother's tail,
and they went home through the trees.

First published in Great Britain in 1992 by
The Bodley Head Children's Books
an imprint of The Random Century Group Ltd
20 Vauxhall Bridge Road, London SW1V 2SA
First published in the U.S.A. in 1991 by
Macmillan Publishing Company, New York

A CIP catalogue record of this book
is available from The British Library

ISBN 0 370 31645 2